For Mom & Pad, Kathy, Connie, Ainsley & Hunter

First Print Run 2015

Made in Canada

The Golden Circle Commando Fairies and the Battle for Dreams

Written by Andrew Stewart
Illustrated by Rob Langille

The moon shone bright in the sky, and from the stars spiraled down the Golden Circle Fairies in a tornado fashion. Headed by Sapphire and Ruby, her second-in-command close behind, they landed swiftly as a jet and as light as a dandelion puff.

The Golden Circle was an elite-trained team of Fairies from Fairyville that had been sent to steal the dreams of children to expand their growing lands.

They would sneak through drain pipes, come through cracks in windows and come down chimneys into the house. There was always a way into the house, in hopes to capture dreams of ponies and giant lollipops.

Tonight the squad accessed by the drain pipes; Sapphire signaled the way and in a whisper directed, "Stay low and in the shadows".

Sneaking silently through the labyrinth of plumbing, out they popped in bubbles from the shower head.

Floating down the hallway, they had only been spotted by The Pook, the household cat, who in his own right was a mighty hunter. But with a quick glance up and a loud "Rrraww," he pushed his head back under his paws.

Sapphire spoke to Ruby in a hushed voice, "Always watch a cat, especially the ones that appear to have no agenda."

The Fairies were obviously not enough of a challenge. Ruby thought to herself, "This cat isn't going to give us any trouble."

Sapphire already had her eye on the prize.

As they approached the open bedroom door the Fairies popped their bubbles and glided into the room. Sarah was snug in her bed dreaming of rainbows, fields of jelly beans and a giant merry-go-round that would be perfect for Fairyville's main square.

Sapphire pulled back the lever of the DREAM EXTRACTOR DE-74 forcing a large bubble out of the end, surrounding Sarah's head.

Just as the music started to play on the merry-go-round, out sucked her dreams and the Fairies surfed back to Fairyville on Sarah's very own rainbow singing their little Fairy song:

The Golden Circle had completed another successful extraction, exchanging high fives and fluttering their wings together in celebration.

Sapphire turned back and looked up the rainbow to see The Pook, the family cat skating in an out-of-control frenzy towards Fairyville.

Sapphire screamed out, "You can never forget the cat! How did that cat get onto our rainbow?" It no longer mattered, nor could they stop him. Sapphire quickly briefed Ruby on a quick defense strategy in hopes to stop The Pook in his tracks.

It is a little known fact that Fairies and cats do not get along. Cats are the true defenders of children's dreams and that is why you often find them snuggled around your head, ready to swat away those pesky winged fairies.

The Pook always hoping, that on a good night perhaps to enjoy one as a tasty treat, as Fairies are the most delicious of the mythical creatures; well at least next to Ogres, but The Pook seldom comes across an Ogre anymore.

It had been since 1942 that a cat, the furious P. Willikers, who had devils in her eyes, claws of razors and speed faster than any Fairy could fly, had even been able to break through into Fairyville. That was a day that Fairy Fables are based on that gives the Fairies their very own nightmares.

Now The Pook was not that sort of cat. He was very reserved; a cat that would enjoy a warm glass of milk and a newspaper at the end of the day.

However, life had dealt him cards that had taken him to the deepest and darkest places in the world. He was not the sort of cat to see his precious Sarah's dreams be sucked away by some pretentious commando Fairies!

At the end of the rainbow, the Fairies had positioned a row of gumball machines.

The Pook launched into the air, screaming a mighty battle cry!

Sapphire dropped her arm, and the Fairies pulled down on the levers allowing gumballs to go rolling everywhere! On top of them was The Pook who's battle cry had turned into a groan. He landed with his paws in the air, contrary to the old adage that cats always land on their feet.

Thankfully, the fact that cats have 9 lives holds true and had served him on more than one occasion. Actually it was 4 occasions if anyone is counting.

The Pook quickly recovered and in a whirlwind of leaps, bounds and directive swats, corralled the Golden Circle into a neat little pile.

He took that merry-go-round from the centre of Fairyville placing it on his head and wrapped the rainbow around his neck. The Pook had Sapphire and her commando Fairies dismantle the stolen dreams to be returned to the children.

Then in a monumental move, had the Fairies fly him back to Sarah pulling him in a royal carriage. He ate jelly beans as a nice travel treat, in lieu of the scrumptious Fairies.

The Pook arrived back before the crack of dawn allowing Sarah to enjoy the last of her dream before waking. He snuggled down in the hallway knowing now that the children would soon wake up, that their dreams would be safe and that he could sleep the rest of the day after another adventurous night.

The End

Andrew Stewart

Rob Langille

Andrew is a children's author, father, husband, and explorer. He is dedicated to the craft of storytelling and bringing children the next big adventure!

Rob is a family man who loves to spend time drawing and playing with his toy cars and wrestlers. He is all about entertaining everybody he meets.

Also Available from Andrew and Rob:

There Is A Boy On Top Of My Bed!
isbn: 978-1461137207

Stanley the Leaf Pile
isbn: 978-1468055559

49029120R00015

Made in the USA
Charleston, SC
16 November 2015